THE BIG
SNEEZE

For my father, Hugh Antonsen

A Red Fox Book. Published by Random House Children's Books
20 Vauxhall Bridge Road, London SW1V 2SA

A division of Random House UK Ltd. London Melbourne Sydney
Auckland Johannesburg and agencies throughout the world

First published by Andersen Press Limited 1985
Beaver edition 1986. Red Fox edition 1993

7 9 10 8

© Ruth Brown 1985

Printed in Singapore

RANDOM HOUSE UK Limited Reg. No. 954009

THE BIG SNEEZE
Ruth Brown

RED FOX

One hot afternoon, the farmer and
his animals were dozing in the barn. The
only sound was the buzz-buzz of a lazy fly.

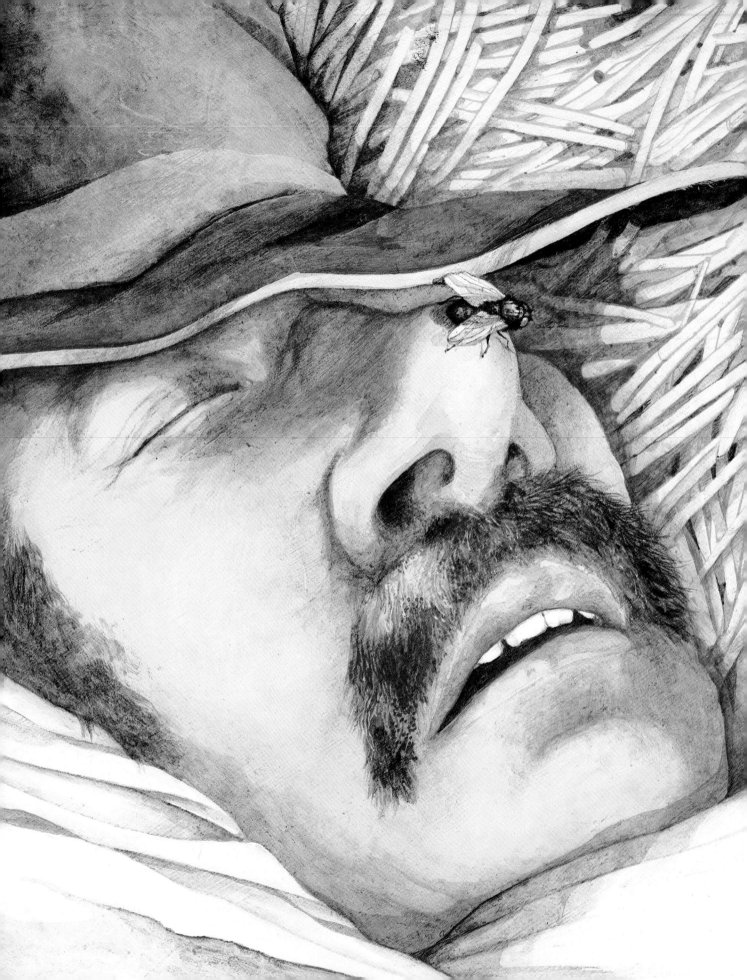

Suddenly the buzzing stopped –
the fly had landed right on the end of the farmer's nose!

"ATISHOOOOOOOOOOO!" the farmer sneezed so hard
that the fly was blown high up into a spider's web.

This disturbed the spider,
who captured the fly –

which alerted the sparrow,
who chased the spider.

This wakened the cat,
who leapt at the bird –

which woke the dog,
and frightened the rats –

who fled from the barn,
chased by the dog –

which scattered the startled
hens from their roost –

and panicked the terrified donkey!

"Nothing, my dear," replied the farmer. "I only sneezed!"